THE BEAR DETECTIVES

The Ghost Train

Written by **SALLY GRINDLEY**

Illustrated by **JO BROWN**

ORCHARD BOOKS

Constable Tiggs

Sergeant Bumble

Charlie's mother

Charlie

"It's the village fair today," said
Sergeant Bumble one morning.

"Can we go on the rides?" asked
Constable Tiggs excitedly.
"We shall be too busy being
detectives," said Bumble sternly.

They walked out onto the green, which was crowded with villagers. "Steady there," said Sergeant Bumble to a young bear who nearly knocked him over.

"Say sorry to Mr Bumble,
Charlie," said the bear's mother.
"Sorry, Mr Bumble," said Charlie.

"Are you going on any of the rides?" asked Charlie.

"I'm afraid we have more important things to do," said Bumble.

"Poor Mr Bumble," said Charlie as
he skipped away, his mother trying
to keep up with him.

"I wish we could go on the
bumper cars," said Tiggs.
"We've got a car of our own,"
said Bumble.

They passed the whirling teacups.
"They look fun," said Tiggs.
"A cup of tea would be better,"
said Bumble.

When they came to the big wheel,
Bumble stood underneath and
said, "Of course, you would have
to be silly to go on that."

They had just reached the cake
stall, when they heard a loud cry.

Charlie's mother came
rushing over to them.
"Oh, Mr Bumble," she sobbed.
"It's my Charlie, I can't find
him anywhere!"

"Where did you last see him?"
asked Bumble.

"We were watching the duck race,
and when I looked round
he had gone."

"Don't worry, madam. My young
constable and I will soon find him."

"He's wearing a red hat," said Tiggs. "If we go up on the big wheel, we should be able to spot him."

Bumble looked horrified. "We're not – I don't – I mean it's a long way up there," he stuttered.

"Come on, Sir," said Tiggs.
"There's no time to lose."
Tiggs grabbed his hand,
pulled him over to the big
wheel and pushed him into
an open pod.

"Up we go!" Tiggs
shouted to the operator.

The wheel began to turn.
Up and up they went.
Bumble closed
his eyes tight.

"The view's fantastic, Sir," said Tiggs. Then suddenly he cried, "I can see Charlie, Sir!"

"Keep an eye on him then," Bumble groaned.

As soon as the pod reached the ground, Tiggs leapt off. Bumble stumbled behind him.

"He's heading for that tent over there," Tiggs called.

They ran after him into the tent.

It was full of mirrors. "Hey, look at me," chuckled Tiggs, standing in front of one of them. "I'm really tall."

"I'm not that fat!" protested
Bumble when he saw himself in
one mirror.

They couldn't find Charlie anywhere, but when they went outside again, Tiggs spotted him heading for the ghost train.

"Not the ghost train," groaned Bumble.

They arrived just in time to jump
into the last wagon.
"Full steam ahead!" called
the driver.

A spider's web
brushed against
Bumble's face.
"Aargh!" he yelled.

A ghost swooped
in front of him.
"Eeek!" he
screamed.

A skeleton jabbed
a finger in his belly.
"Get me out of
here!" he bellowed.

"It's all right, Sir," said Tiggs.
"They're not real."
The train came back out into the
light. Standing on the platform
were Charlie and his mother.

"Now, Charlie, say sorry to
Mr Bumble for all the trouble
you've caused," Charlie's mother
said gently.

"Sorry, Mr Bumble," said Charlie.
"Have you had a nice day?"
"Ha, yes, of course," blustered Bumble.
"Now, try not to get lost again."

Charlie skipped away,
his mother still trying
to keep up with him.

"Well, Constable Tiggs," said Bumble,
"after our fine piece of detective
work, I think we've had enough
of fairs for one day, don't you?"

"Yes, Sir," smiled Tiggs. "I'll make
you a nice cup of tea."

THE BEAR DETECTIVES

SALLY GRINDLEY 🎩 JO BROWN

Bucket Rescue	978 1 84616 160 5
Who Shouted Boo?	978 1 84616 159 9
The Ghost Train	978 1 84616 161 2
Treasure Hunt	978 1 84616 158 2
The Mysterious Earth	978 1 84616 163 6
The Strange Pawprint	978 1 84616 164 3
The Missing Spaghetti	978 1 84616 165 0
A Very Important Day	978 1 84616 162 9

All priced at £4.99

Orchard Colour Crunchies are available from all good bookshops,
or can be ordered direct from the publisher:
Orchard Books, PO BOX 29, Douglas IM99 1BQ
Credit card orders please telephone 01624 836000
or fax 01624 837033 or visit our website: www.orchardbooks.co.uk
or e-mail: bookshop@enterprise.net for details.

To order please quote title, author and ISBN
and your full name and address.
Cheques and postal orders should be made payable to 'Bookpost plc.'
Postage and packing is FREE within the UK
(overseas customers should add £2.00 per book).

Prices and availability are subject to change.